BIG CHAPTER BOOKS

The Berenstain Bears
in the

WAX MUSEUM

by the Berenstains

A BIG CHAPTER BOOK™

Random House New York

Copyright © 1999 by Berenstain Enterprises, Inc.

All rights reserved under International and Pan-American Copyright Conventions. Published in the United States by Random House, Inc., New York, and simultaneously in Canada by Random House of Canada Limited, Toronto.

www.randomhouse.com/kids

www.berenstainbears.com

Library of Congress Cataloging-in-Publication Data
Berenstain, Stan, 1923–
The Berenstain Bears in the wax museum / Stan & Jan Berenstain.
p. cm. — (A big chapter book)
SUMMARY: Brother Bear and his cousin Fred get more excitement than they had hoped for when they become involved in the efforts to build an entertainment complex, including a wax museum, in Beartown.
ISBN 0-679-88947-7 (trade) — ISBN 0-679-98947-1 (lib. bdg.)
[1. Bears—Fiction. 2. Adventure and adventurers—Fiction.
3. Criminals—Fiction.] I. Berenstain, Jan, 1923– . II. Title.
III. Series: Berenstain, Stan, 1923– . Big chapter book.
PZ7.B4483Berkw 1999
[Fic]—dc21
99-12686

Printed in the United States of America—10 9 8 7 6 5 4 3 2 1

RANDOM HOUSE and colophon are registered trademarks of Random House, Inc. BIG CHAPTER BOOKS and colophon are trademarks of Berenstain Enterprises, Inc.

Contents

Chapter 1
The Good Old Days

Every spring, when Bear Country School let out for summer vacation, cubs' hopes were sky-high. Whether they planned to be at home or at camp, most of them expected to have a great time. But summer was a funny thing. It had a way of turning out to be not quite as great as you'd expected.

That was often the case for Brother Bear. And he was a summer bear if ever there was one. He liked school well enough. But summer meant fun, excitement, adventure. Of course, Brother's best friend, Bonnie Brown, wasn't usually around in the summertime. She lived at Grizzly Mansion with her aunt and uncle, Lady and Squire Grizzly, during the school year, but often went out to Hollywood for the summer to act in TV commercials and sitcoms and spend time with her movie actor and actress parents.

Fortunately for Brother, though, he could always count on good old Cousin Fred to

keep him from getting too bored in the summertime. He and Fred went way back. When they were babies, they played together in the same playpen in Brother's backyard in the summertime. When they were toddlers, they were inseparable in their summer play-group.

But it was when Brother and Fred were old enough to go to Bear Country School that the summers really started to heat up, so to speak. They had all kinds of summer adventures together: running races, playing softball, fishing, hiking, going to Grizzlyland Amusement Park, and snooping around in

places they weren't supposed to be—like Farmer Ben's hayloft.

And this summer won't be any different, Brother thought as he walked home from the last half-day of school. He was going to phone Fred right away to make plans for the afternoon. But he never had the chance, because Fred beat him to it.

Fred, who was known to read the dictionary for fun, never used words he couldn't define. "Premonition," he said. "A feeling of anticipation about a future event."

"Okay," said Brother. "So what's your premonition?"

"You know how we always said that summer is for adventure?" said Fred.

"Sure," said Brother. "And it's true. When's a better time for adventure?"

"But we always end up doing the same things summer after summer," said Fred.

"Fishing, hiking, Grizzlyland, and all that stuff. The same adventures. Well, I had a premonition that we're gonna have a new adventure this summer. Just you and me. And it'll be more than an adventure with a small a. It'll be a Great Adventure—you know, the kind with a capital G and a capital A."

"What kind of Great Adventure?" asked Brother.

"Dunno," said Fred. "That's where the premonition left off."

"Well, I don't know about any Great Adventure," said Brother. "But I have a premonition that you and I are gonna do something this afternoon."

"You must be psychic," said Fred. "But why wait till this afternoon? We could go downtown for lunch right now."

"Deal," said Brother. "Burger Bear or Pizza Shack?"

"Let's decide when I come by and pick you up," said Fred. "See ya…"

As the cubs got ready to go out, neither of them had the slightest idea that their Great Adventure would begin that very day. In fact, it would begin before they even had a chance to eat lunch…

Chapter 2
Dullsville

Minutes later, Brother and Fred were walking through downtown Beartown on their way to the Pizza Shack for lunch. As they strolled through the town square, someone called to them from the bench in front of Old Shag, Beartown's historic back-scratching tree. It was Grizzly Gramps.

"Hey, you two," said Gramps, rising. "Wait up. I just happen to be headed in the same direction you are."

Now, Brother and Fred usually liked to run into Gramps. Gramps was one of their favorite bears in all Bear Country. But today was different. For one thing, their stomachs were already growling, and Gramps was one of Beartown's slowest walkers. If he walked them to the Pizza Shack, they might faint from hunger before they got there! For another thing, even supposing they didn't

faint from hunger on their way to the Pizza Shack, what if Gramps invited himself to have lunch with them? After all, this was their very first day of summer buddyhood, and in that kind of situation—well, two's company and three's a crowd, as the saying goes.

"Beautiful day, eh?" said Gramps as they began inching their way down the sidewalk. "What are you cubs up to?"

"Pizza Shack," said Brother. "We're starving."

Gramps noticed that both cubs looked a little tense. They were staring straight ahead, as if they were afraid of what he might say next. He chuckled and said, "Oh, don't worry. I'm not gonna invite myself to have lunch with you. And I'll only walk with you as far as Grizzly Avenue."

The cubs relaxed.

"Bet I know where you're headed afterward," Gramps said. "The same place I'm headed now. The Bearsonian Institution."

Brother shook his head. "Why would we want to go to the Bearsonian, Gramps?" he said. "We've been there at least a million times."

"Didn't you know?" said Gramps. "There's a special exhibit on the Great Bear War in the Hall of Bear Country History. This week only."

"We're going out to Birder's Woods for a hike," said Fred. "Then, if there's time, we'll play some catch at the schoolyard."

"You mean you came all the way downtown just to have lunch?" said Gramps. "That seems kinda odd."

"No, it doesn't," said Brother. "There's nothing to do in this town, anyway. Except eat pizza."

"Or burgers," added Fred. He had wanted to go to the Burger Bear for lunch, but Brother had held out for pizza.

"You gotta be kiddin'," said Gramps. "What about takin' in a matinee at the Bearjou Theater?"

"The Bearjou's an old dump," said Fred. "It doesn't even have cup holders."

"And it never runs the kind of movies we like," said Brother.

"Such as what?" asked Gramps.

"Such as weird sci-fi thrillers and creepy, disgusting horror movies," said Brother.

"Yeah!" said Fred. "Like *Invasion of the Bruin Snatchers* and *The Eyeballs from Outer Space.*"

"Thank goodness for that," Gramps muttered to himself. Then, to the cubs, he said, "I guess you have a real gripe there."

"You bet we do," said Brother. "I'm tellin' you, Gramps, this place is Dullsville. Right, Fred?"

Fred was about to nod in agreement, but suddenly he stopped walking and stared straight ahead. Somehow they had reached the corner of Bruin Street and Grizzly Avenue without noticing the long fence just across the street. "Hey, that's new," said Fred. "What's it all about?"

The fence was painted in all kinds of bright, jazzy colors with the words: WATCH THIS SPACE FOR THE MOST EXCITING DEVELOPMENT IN THE HISTORY OF BEARTOWN!

"Hmm," said Gramps. "Don't know what it's all about. But whatever it is, it sure doesn't look like it belongs in 'Dullsville.'"

They crossed the street and sidled up to the fence. Brother peered through a crack, but all he could see was a bunch of building materials piled and stacked in various places. He turned to Gramps and said, "Maybe it'll be something really cool!"

But Gramps had already decided it wouldn't be. Gramps wasn't a big fan of change, especially when it happened in the town he'd grown up in and lived in all his life. "I doubt it," he muttered. "Probably one of them big ol' chain stores that sells everything a bear doesn't need. Like Bearmart or Bears Roebuck. The kind that chases all the little mom-and-pop stores out of town."

"Not likely," said Fred. "They don't use Day-Glo paint to announce new Bearmarts. But I guess we'll find out soon enough."

"'Fraid so," said Gramps. "Hey, why don't you cubs meet me at the Bearsonian after lunch? I can show you around the special exhibit."

Brother was tempted to say yes. Gramps may have been a slow walker, but he could be a real fast talker. And an interesting one, too. The Great Bear War was kind of a hobby of his. He knew everything there was to know about it. He could tell you about all the famous battles, and about the lives of the great generals, like Ulysses S. Bear and Grizzwall Jackson. He even knew the Gettysbear Address by heart.

But then Brother remembered that this was the first day in quite a while that he and Fred had had a chance to spend time together—just the two of them. So he said, "Thanks, Gramps, maybe next time."

"Okay, you two," said Gramps. "But remember: this week only..." And he ambled off down Grizzly Avenue in the direction of the Bearsonian.

Chapter 3
Dullsville No More?

Brother and Fred spent several days hiking, fishing, and playing catch before they decided it was high time to take another look at the mysterious building project on the corner of Bruin Street and Grizzly Avenue. Maybe construction had already begun. And maybe they could figure out what it was all about.

As they approached the corner of Bruin and Grizzly, the cubs could see that things were progressing. Or, rather, they could hear that things were progressing. From behind the multi-colored fence came the sounds of high-powered digging equipment

and cement mixers. Then they noticed a new sign on top of the fence. It read: AT LAST! EXCITEMENT COMES TO BEARTOWN! A FABULOUS ENTERTAINMENT CENTER GOING UP ON THIS SITE!

Brother and Fred looked at each other in astonishment. "An entertainment center?" said Fred. "In Beartown? I must be dreaming. Pinch me." Brother obliged. "Ouch! Hey, I'm not dreaming!"

"Come on, let's have a look," said Brother.

They raced across the street to peer through the cracks in the fence. They saw huge mechanical scoops and shovels lifting and hauling dirt from a vast hole in the ground. A fleet of cement mixers was lined up alongside, churning merrily away.

"They're getting ready to lay the foundation," said Fred.

"Wow! Whatever it is, it's gonna be huge!"

With their noses pressed against the fence, the cubs traded guesses about what the new entertainment center would be like. Maybe it would be an amusement park with cool rides and a funhouse. Or maybe a sports center with miniature golf and an arena for rollerblading. Or an enormous arcade, with every kind of pinball machine

and electronic game ever invented. Or a multiplex cinema, with twenty screens and shops and cafés. Or a huge theme restaurant, all made up like a rain forest or a prince's palace or a haunted mansion...

The possibilities seemed endless. They couldn't wait to find out which one it would turn out to be!

Fortunately, they didn't have to wait long. Just until later that afternoon, in fact. When

Brother got home from rollerblading with Fred, he found Papa relaxing in his easy chair in the living room. That afternoon's *Beartown Gazette* lay folded neatly on his lap.

"Papa," said Brother, "have you seen anything in the paper about the new entertainment center that's going up downtown?"

"Entertainment center?" said Papa. "You mean that thing with the Day-Glo fence at

Bruin and Grizzly? Gramps told me about it, but he didn't say anything about it being an entertainment center. Oh, the paper? Nothing so far. But I haven't checked today's yet." When he unfolded the paper and had a look, his eyebrows shot up. "Well, well," he said. "Have a look at this."

Papa turned the paper around so that Brother could read the top headline. It said:

MADAME BEARSAUD'S FAMOUS WAX MUSEUM
COMES TO BEARTOWN.

"Awesome!" cried Brother so loudly that it brought Mama out of the kitchen and Sister down the stairs. "Go ahead, Papa, read the article!"

Papa cleared his throat and read, " 'Madame Bearsaud—' "

"You say it *Bear-so,* dear, not *Bear-sawd,*" interrupted Mama.

"Oh," said Papa. "Must be a misprint. Anyway, here's what it says:

" 'Madame Bearsaud, the world-famous owner of Madame Bearsaud's Wax Museums, is building a new branch of her entertainment empire right in the middle of Beartown. Not only will the wax museum be larger than the one in Big Bear City, but attached to it will be an old-fashioned movie palace, called the Screaming Room, that will show only horror and sci-fi movies. Also attached will be a theme restaurant, Chez Bearsaud, where diners will be served by waiters dressed like the famous monsters, villains, and heroes in the wax museum. Of particular interest in the museum itself will be the statue of Queen Elizabear, adorned with priceless replicas of the great queen's crown jewels.

" 'Never before has a business of this type or size been located in Beartown, but the Beartown zoning board has given Madame Bearsaud the go-ahead to build on the vacant lot at the corner of Bruin Street and Grizzly Avenue. The board's vote was two to one in favor of Madame Bearsaud, with Mayor Honeypot and Farmer Ben voting yes and Lady Grizzly voting no.' "

Papa looked up from the paper and smiled at Brother and Sister. "Well, cubs, what do you have to say about that?"

"Hurray for Madame Bearsaud!" cried Sister.

"And hurray for the Beartown zoning board!" added Brother.

Chapter 4
Lady Grizzly's Challenge

But the cubs' hurrays weren't the last word on the subject. Mama shook her head and said, "The new entertainment center certainly sounds exciting, but one thing worries me: Lady Grizzly's no vote."

"Who cares about Lady Grizzly's no vote?" said Papa. "She lost fair and square, two to one. Case closed."

"I understand that," said Mama. "But it's more what the vote represents than the vote itself that worries me."

"You're talking in riddles, dear," Papa complained.

"Yeah," said Sister. "What do you mean, Mama?"

"Just this," said Mama. "That single no vote represents an anti–Madame Bearsaud attitude that I expect is shared by some other Beartown folks. Mark my word: there will be protests against the new entertainment center. And it's quite possible that one of the other members of the zoning board will change his vote."

"Oh, my goodness," said Papa. "Mama's right."

"I don't get it," said Brother. "Why would anyone be against the entertainment center?"

"You'd understand if you were a grown-up," said Papa. "Why, I can just picture Lady Grizzly complaining to the squire: 'A wax museum? How vulgar! How tawdry! All those awful wax statues of monsters and villains will corrupt Beartown's cubs...' "

And if truth be told, across town, in Squire Grizzly's study, Lady Grizzly was at that very moment complaining to her husband. "A wax museum?" she was saying.

"How vulgar! How tawdry! All those awful wax statues of monsters and villains will corrupt Beartown's cubs! Dear, we must stop this Madame Bearsaud from completing her infernal project!"

Squire Grizzly, sitting behind his big wooden desk, shrugged and shook his head. "But I don't see what we can do about it, dear," he said. "After all, the zoning board has already voted—"

"Nonsense!" snapped Lady Grizzly. "The zoning board, as you well know, is perfectly free to change its vote within a month if it sees fit. And to have it do just that, I shall organize an anti–Madame Bearsaud campaign the likes of which our sleepy little town has never seen!"

"But, dear," said the squire, "think of the boost the new center will give to the Beartown businesses that I own. Madame

Bearsaud's will put Beartown on the map. Folks from all over Bear Country will flock to town, and Madame Bearsaud's theme restaurant won't even begin to be able to serve all of them. The overflow will wind up in my Burger Bear and my Pizza Shack. And they'll wind up shopping in Grizzworth's, my five-and-dime store, and at 8-Twelve, my convenience store. Furthermore, Madame Bearsaud has taken out a handsome loan from my bank, Great Grizzly National, to finance her project, and the interest she pays on that loan will provide us with a steady stream of money for years and years to come—"

"Not another word!" shouted Lady Grizzly. "Money, money, money! Is that all you care about in life?"

The squire was silent for a moment.

"Well?" prodded his wife.

"Hold on," mumbled the squire. "I'm thinking it over…"

"Humph!" said Lady Grizzly, stalking from the room. "I've heard quite enough from you!"

Lady Grizzly marched into the drawing room and went straight to the telephone. First she'd call Mrs. Ben, then Mrs. Honeypot. And when they got through with Farmer Ben and Mayor Honeypot, those two would wish they'd never heard of the Beartown zoning board!

Chapter 5
ABATE vs. BAD?

Later that evening, the phone rang in the Bears' living room, where the Bear family was watching television. Mama answered. "Oh, hello, Lady Grizzly," she said. "Oh, no, you're not interrupting anything. We were just watching *Bear Country's Funniest*

Home Videos, but it's a rerun. Yes…uh-huh…I see…but before you go any further, Lady Grizzly, I should tell you that Papa and I are not really against the new entertainment center. Thank you, anyway. That's quite all right. Goodbye."

Mama replaced the receiver and looked up with a sly smile. "Well," she said, "what did I tell you? Lady Grizzly has already organized an anti–Madame Bearsaud campaign. Her new group is called ABATE. It stands for All Bears Against Tacky Entertainment."

"Humph!" said Papa. "She oughta call it ABAF. All Bears Against Fun!"

"Right on!" cried Brother and Sister in unison.

"Not so fast, you three," said Mama. "Lady Grizzly is just worried about the effect of the new center on cubs."

"Baloney!" said Papa. "She's just worried about her own stuck-up ideas about what's in good taste and what isn't!"

"Well," said Mama, "that may be part of it, too. But it isn't just Lady Grizzly now. Mrs. Ben and Mrs. Honeypot have already joined ABATE. And you know what that means…"

"Oh, no!" groaned Papa. "That means they're gonna try to get Ben and the mayor to change their votes…Hmm. I'm not worried about the mayor. He'll do whatever he thinks will get him re-elected, no matter what Mrs. Honeypot thinks. But Farmer Ben—that's a different story altogether. He's liable to crack under the pressure…"

"And you know what Mrs. Ben is like when she gets a bee in her bonnet," said Brother. "Talk about pressure!"

"Hey, you two!" scolded Mama. "That's

not very nice."

"You know what they say," said Papa. " 'Nice guys finish last.' We're gonna get a counter-campaign going—in favor of Madame Bearsaud. And we'll call it…what should we call it, cubs?"

"I know!" said Brother. "BAD. Bears Against Dullsville."

"Yeah!" said Sister. "We can have T-shirts printed up that say WE BAD!"

"I don't know," said Mama, shaking her head. "That might put off a lot of folks…"

Chapter 6
The Truckers Cometh

Mama was right about BAD, of course. But it didn't matter. As usual, Papa was mostly hot air: all talk, no action. And the cubs quickly forgot all about trying to fight Lady Grizzly's campaign. They didn't really believe she would be successful. They were so in love with the idea of Madame Bearsaud's

Wax Museum and Entertainment Center that they couldn't really imagine it not coming true.

Meanwhile, Brother and Fred continued their summer of adventure. And Madame Bearsaud's entertainment center was now at the center of their adventures. In fact, it seemed on the verge of becoming the Great Adventure Fred had dreamed of. As the days of construction wore on, the cubs hatched a scheme to sneak into Madame Bearsaud's for a look-see. It would be a huge thrill to see what was inside before anyone else did. And an even bigger thrill to report their exploits to the rest of Beartown's admiring cubs. All that was left to do was choose the right moment.

That moment came sooner than they expected. Work on the center had speeded up lately. Perhaps Madame Bearsaud had got wind of ABATE's campaign and decided that an early completion of the center would put a stop to it. But whatever the reason for the speed-up, the massive building was finished in a matter of days, and now trucks labeled MADAME BEARSAUD'S WAX MUSEUM began coming and going through the gateway in the multi-colored fence.

"Do you think they're bringing in the wax

statues?" Brother asked Fred as they stood watching from across the street.

"If I were a betting bear," said Fred, "I'd give you a hundred-to-one odds that they are."

"Well," said Brother, "what are we waiting for? The time for our Great Adventure is upon us!"

Fred smiled, and across the street they went.

Chapter 7
No Trespassing

Brother and Fred crept along the alleyway behind the building project, staying close to the fence. They were looking for a break or hole in the fence in a spot where they wouldn't be seen sneaking in. And sure enough, they found one: a crack in the fence just wide enough for a cub to slip through.

Brother was ready to go for it, but Fred held back. "Are you sure we should be doing this?" he said. He pointed to a sign just above the crack in the fence. It read: NO TRESPASSING.

"Hmm," said Brother. "Trespassing. That's an awful big word, and I'm just a cub." He winked. "I don't know what it means. Do you?"

Now, Brother hadn't forgotten that Fred liked to read the dictionary for fun. But he expected his wink to do the trick. And it did. Fred suddenly lost his memory for long words.

"Trespassing," he said, scratching his head. "I'm not sure...I think it's a fancy word for fishing."

"Oh," said Brother. " 'No fishing.' Well, that's no sweat. We didn't even bring our fishing poles, did we? Come on, let's go."

No one could possibly have seen the cubs dart from the crack in the fence to a back door that was propped open with a garbage can. Before you could sneeze, they were inside the building. It was very dark. From the little bit of daylight coming through the propped-open door, they could see that they were in an enormous room, like a huge cavern.

"Wow," said Fred, peering around. "Whatever it is, it's a whole lot bigger than the school auditorium…"

"It must be the Screaming Room," said Brother. "You know—the horror movie palace."

"Of course!" said Fred. "Whoa, what's that?"

Brother felt Fred press against him, trembling. When he looked up to where Fred was pointing, he got a little trembly

himself. But as his eyes got used to the darkness, he relaxed. "It's just the balcony," he said.

"But it's also Bearzilla, the monster!" cried Fred. "It's like he's holding up the balcony!"

"Cool!" said Brother. "And that's not all. Look at the walls. Murals all over 'em!"

"Bearcula!" said Fred. "And the Frankenbear Monster!"

"And the Wolf Bear!" said Brother.

"I can't take this," said Fred. "Let's get

out of here!" He made a move for the propped-open door, but Brother grabbed his arm. "Lemme go!" protested Fred.

"We can't turn back now," Brother scolded. He pointed at a rectangle outlined by yellow light under a red-glowing exit sign. "Look. There's a side door. It must lead into another part of the building. I say we check it out."

"And I still say we get out of here—" Fred started to say.

But just then, the cubs heard the high-pitched beeping of a truck backing up to the propped-open door. Its shadow deepened the darkness in the Screaming Room.

"On second thought," said Fred, "let's check out that side door…"

The cubs hurried to the exit and slipped through into a dimly lit hallway. On the wall before them were the words WAX MUSEUM,

with an arrow pointing to an exit at the far end of the hallway.

"All right!" said Brother. "Now we're in business!"

"Not exactly," said Fred, still a little trembly. "Madame Bearsaud's in business. We're trespassing!"

"No, we're not," said Brother with another wink. "We forgot our trespassing

poles, remember? Come on."

When the cubs went through the far exit into the wax museum, they almost panicked. The brighter light blinded them for an instant, and they could hear the sounds of workbears moving heavy objects. Fortunately, Brother spied an old barrel lying on its side in the nearest corner. They hurried over to it and crept inside.

"You think they saw us?" whispered Fred.

"Nah," said Brother. "We're in great shape. This is the perfect hiding place."

"Sure, it's a great hiding place," whispered Fred. "But we can't see anything!"

"Oh, yeah?" said Brother. "Check out this little knothole…"

Sure enough, there was a tiny knothole in the barrel wall right at eye level. And it faced out into the wax museum.

"Cool," said Brother, peering through the hole. "Here come some workbears carrying something. It's a wax statue in a fancy gown… I bet that's Queen Elizabear."

"Let me see," said Fred, pressing one of the lenses of his glasses against the knothole. "They've put Queen Elizabear right in the middle of the room. Hey, wait a minute—if that's Queen Elizabear, where are her crown jewels?"

"Madame Bearsaud probably keeps them in a safe when the museum's closed," said Brother.

"Oh, right," said Fred. "Hey, there are other statues out there; the workbears must have brought them in before we got here. Blackbear the Pirate! He's holding a cutlass...and Bearjamin Franklin's holding a kite...and—uh-oh, they must have dropped one of the wax figures. It's lying flat on its back!"

"Let's see," said Brother. "Oh, that's Gullibear."

"Gullibear?" said Fred.

"You know, from *Gullibear's Travels*," said Brother. "He's supposed to be flat on his back. See? The Lillibruins have tied him down with rope. Here come the workbears with another statue...Cool! It's the Frankenbear Monster! Hmm..."

"What is it?" said Fred.

"Those three workbears," said Brother. "They look familiar...I can't really see their

faces, though. But I just got a pretty good look at their supervisor—he's the one barking all the orders—and he looks kind of familiar, too…Never mind, my eyes must be playing tricks on me. But this is awesome, Fred! Just think: we're the first bears in town to see this!"

Just then Fred said, "Uh-oh. Look what I found."

Fred pointed to some words that had been carved into the inside of the barrel. Brother let out a groan. The carving read: TOO-TALL WAS HERE.

Chapter 8
The Too-Tall Seal of Approval

Once they had exited Madame Bearsaud's the way they'd entered, Brother and Fred hurried to the schoolyard, hoping to find some cubs to tell about their exploits. The schoolyard was always a good place for sports during summer vacation, and, sure enough, a softball game was in progress on one of the diamonds. Too-Tall and his gang were playing a team that included Barry Bruin and Gil Grizzwold. Too-Tall was at bat.

"Hey, big guy!" called Brother. "We just saw your name carved in a barrel!"

Too-Tall dropped the bat and came over,

the others following. "You two snuck into Madame Bearsaud's?" he said. "Nice work."

"Wait a minute, boss," said Skuzz. "They could be lyin'."

"Yeah," said Smirk. "How do we know they really snuck in?"

"Because I didn't tell nobody about

carvin' my name in that barrel," said Too-Tall. "Not even you guys."

"Right, boss!" said Vinnie. "That means these two are the real thing!"

"Hey, boss," said Skuzz. "How 'bout we invite 'em to Madame Bearsaud's grand opening with us?"

Brother and Fred beamed with pride. Too-Tall and the gang may have been jerks and bullies a lot of the time, but it still felt good to be accepted by cubs with tough-guy reputations.

"Well, it's okay with me if they tag along," said Too-Tall. "Except for one thing. There may not *be* a grand opening."

"What?" said Barry Bruin. "Why not?"

"Because Mayor Honeypot just called a special session of the zoning board for tomorrow afternoon," said Too-Tall. "The word's out that Mrs. Ben strong-armed

Farmer Ben into changing his vote. And you know what that means."

"Yeah," said Gil Grizzwold gloomily. "No Madame Bearsaud's in Beartown."

"We gotta do somethin', boss!" said Smirk.

"Yeah!" said Vinnie. "We can't let that ABATE gang push us around!"

"For once I agree with you boneheads," said Too-Tall. "Now, listen. The meetin's in the town hall, and it's open to the public. I hear Madame Bearsaud herself is gonna be there. And her hunchback assistant, Igor."

"Hunchback assistant?" said Fred. "Hey, this is getting to be like a horror movie."

"Yeah," said Too-Tall. "He's this weird, spooky, bent-over guy. Goes everywhere with Madame Bearsaud."

There were cries of "Cool!" and "Awesome!" from the cubs.

Too-Tall instructed each of them to contact as many friends as possible. His plan was for all of them to show up at the zoning board session and cheer and applaud like crazy every time Madame Bearsaud's name was mentioned. They might not be as well organized as ABATE, but if push came to shove, they could be twice as loud and obnoxious.

Chapter 9
A Strange Turn of Events

The next afternoon, it didn't take long for the town hall's auditorium to fill up with concerned citizens. The members of ABATE, wearing large ABATE buttons, arrived before anyone else and took up the front row of seats. Well, not exactly the whole front row. In fact, they took up just the middle five seats. That's because ABATE had only six members: Lady Grizzly (who was seated on the stage with the other zoning board members), Mrs. Ben, Mrs. Honeypot, Grizzly Gramps, Miss Glitch (Bear Country School's English teacher), and Fred Furry (owner of the Bearjou Theater).

Not only were there just six measly members of ABATE, they didn't seem to have any supporters in the rest of the audience. When the mass of cubs started up a chant of "Fun for you and fun for me! Cast your vote for Madame B.!", many of the grownups joined in, and those who didn't join in showed their approval by nodding and smiling.

"Well, well!" said Papa to Mama. "Looks like the Beartown public is solidly behind Madame Bearsaud. That means Mayor Honeypot won't change his vote."

"That's true, dear," said Mama. "But it was Farmer Ben you were worried about, wasn't it?"

"Oh, right," said Papa. "How does he look?"

As the pro–Madame Bearsaud chant filled the auditorium, Farmer Ben sat in his

chair on the stage, looking meekly down at his hands, which were folded in his lap.

"Uh-oh," said Papa. "He looks exactly like a bear who has let his wife talk him into going against the public will and his own conscience."

"That's not fair," said Mama. "Maybe Ben has really changed his mind. Maybe he has better taste than you think."

"Nonsense!" said Papa. "Ben's taste is

every bit as rotten as mine! We used to
hang out together at those tacky traveling
carnivals when we were young. Ben's a bear
who knows how important bad taste is to
cubs growing up."

Brother and Fred, sitting with their
friends, were more concerned with getting
a look at Madame Bearsaud and Igor than
with Farmer Ben. But when Mayor Honeypot stepped up to the microphone on the
podium, the famous duo was still missing.

"Ladles and Gentle Ben—er, I mean, ladies and gentlemen," said the mayor, who tended to get his words mixed up. "We've gathered today for a revote by the boning zord—er, zoning board—on the matter of Madame Bearsaud's Wax Museum and Entertainment Center. In the interests of open public debate, I've scheduled two speakers from the audience—one for and one against. Madame Bearsaud is for, and Miss Glitch is against. Madame Bearsaud doesn't seem to have arrived yet, so at this time I invite Miss Splitch to geek—I mean, Miss Glitch to speak."

Miss Glitch stepped up to the microphone that had been placed at the foot of the stage and addressed the audience. "Ladies and gentlemen. I wish to talk about the issues of morals, values, and good taste…"

"I wish she'd talk about 'em somewhere else," muttered Papa in the audience.

"Shush, dear," whispered Mama.

But by the end of Miss Glitch's long-winded speech, even Mama was rolling her eyes. As the teacher returned to her seat, only the five other members of ABATE applauded.

"Madame Bearsaud seems to be tumwhat sardy—er, somewhat tardy," said Mayor Honeypot. "Perhaps we should wait a bit before we vote." He glanced over at Lady Grizzly, who was glaring at him. "Er, on the other hand, it really isn't fair to hold up an important vote just because a speaker is late. So, to start the voting, I cast my vote in favor of Madame Bearsaud!"

The mayor beamed as cheering and applause filled the auditorium. Then he turned to Farmer Ben. "Ben, how do you vote?"

Farmer Ben cleared his throat but kept looking down at his hands. He appeared to mumble something.

"For the record," said Mayor Honeypot, "Farmer Ben has changed his vote. He has voted against Madame Bearsaud." He held up his hands to discourage the cascade of boos and hisses that followed. "Now, now, folks. Quiet down. There's one more vote to be heard. Of course, that vote belongs to

Lady Grizzly, the leader of ABATE, and I guess we all know how she's gonna vote." He raised his hands again to quiet the boo-birds. "But I have to ask her anyway. Just for the record, Lady Grizzly, how do you vote?"

Lady Grizzly opened her mouth to speak. But at that moment, from the back of the auditorium, came a shout. "Wait!"

All eyes turned to the entrance, where a figure stood wearing an elaborate gown, a fancy hat, and lots of jewelry.

"I'll bet that's Madame Bearsaud!" said Brother.

"And that weird guy lurking behind her must be Igor!" added Fred.

All eyes remained fixed on the two figures as they made their way to the microphone at the front of the auditorium. The bejeweled woman walked slowly and gracefully, her head held high, while her hunched companion followed awkwardly, dragging one foot. When they reached the microphone, the elegant lady spoke loudly and clearly in a foreign accent.

"I am zee great Madame Bearsaud," she said. "And zis is my new assistant, Igor, from zee faraway land of Grizzylvania. He vould say hello to you, but he is mute: he cannot speak."

Igor bowed so low that his nose almost touched the floor, which wasn't hard to do since he was already bent over so far.

"I have come to zis lovely little town," continued Madame Bearsaud, "to bring you zee fame and fortune." She paused until the cheering and clapping died down. "As you must realize, my new vax museum and entertainment center vill be a great boon to zee business district of zis town." Now she looked straight at Fred Furry in the first row. "Even zee lovely old Bearjou Theater vill benefit, since parents from all over zee area vill attend its matinees after dropping zeir cubs off at my horror movie palace. Zank you all very much."

As a great wave of applause swept over Madame Bearsaud and Igor, Fred Furry jumped up and cried, "My gosh, she's

right!" He ripped off his ABATE button and
threw it on the floor, then hurried over to
Madame Bearsaud. "Please, Madame, take
my seat," he said. "Here, let me help you."
He led Madame Bearsaud to his front-row
seat as Mayor Honeypot raised his hands to
quiet the audience.

"Thank you, Badame Mearsaud—er, Madame Bearsaud," said the mayor. "Those are

inspiring words indeed. But let's not forget that Lady Grizzly still has the deciding vote. Well, Lady Grizzly, how do you vote?"

Once again Lady Grizzly opened her mouth to speak. But again she was interrupted by Madame Bearsaud, who suddenly rose and said, "Is that you, Meg?"

Lady Grizzly froze. She stared straight at Madame Bearsaud. "Oh, my goodness!" she cried. "I didn't recognize you in all that makeup and jewelry!"

Lady Grizzly hurried down from the stage. Madame Bearsaud met her at the side of the auditorium. They fell into each other's arms like long-lost friends, which is exactly what they were. The audience was fascinated. Some tried to crowd close to hear what was going on. But fierce, threatening Igor made them keep their distance.

The old friends spoke in hushed voices so as

not to be overheard. "My goodness gracious!" said Lady Grizzly. "Minnie McGrundy! I haven't seen you since we were kicking up our heels together in the chorus line of the

Folies Beargère! When did you become the great Madame Bearsaud?"

"Oh, years ago," said Madame Bearsaud. "And it's been marvelous!" She held Lady Grizzly at arm's length. "Meg Moxie! Just look at you! It took me awhile to recognize you in such beautiful clothes and expensive jewelry. So you're the one who married Squire Grizzly. What have you been doing to keep yourself busy, my dear?"

"Charity work, mostly," said Lady Grizzly. "I'm chairbear of FOTH—Friends of the Hospital. Every year we raise money for Bear Country Memorial Hospital here in Beartown."

"That's wonderful!" said Madame Bearsaud. Then, with the light of an idea in her eyes, she said, "Igor, clear the way to that microphone. I have an announcement to make.

"My dear friends," she said into the microphone. "I hereby pledge all the proceeds from the grand opening of Madame Bearsaud's Wax Museum and Entertainment Center to Friends of the Hospital, Lady Grizzly's marvelous charity!"

"And in honor of this great event," said Lady Grizzly, not to be outdone, "I shall wear my priceless diamond necklace for the first time in public. That should sell a few extra tickets!"

The audience, which had been listening in

stunned silence, broke into wild applause.

Lady Grizzly looked up at Mayor Honey-pot on the stage. "Mr. Mayor," she said, "I wish to change my vote. I now cast my vote in favor of Madame Bearsaud!"

That, of course, made the vote two to one in favor of Madame Bearsaud. The town hall shook from all the cheering and applause. And when the noise finally died down, Farmer Ben changed his vote again to make it unanimous.

Chapter 10
Lingering Suspicions

As Brother and Fred walked home from the town hall, Brother seemed lost in thought. But Fred didn't notice. He was too busy talking.

"What just happened is great, of course," he was saying. "But it's kind of sad, too. Because it means our Great Adventure is pretty much over. Our Great Adventure was watching that building go up and dreaming about what it would be like inside. And sneaking in and seeing all that stuff was the climax. I tell ya, we can't top that. It's like reading an adventure story and realizing you've already read the most exciting chapter. Going to the grand opening will be

cool, but it won't be as good as sneaking in was—or even as good as all the anticipation... Hey, are you listening?"

"Huh?" said Brother.

"I've been telling you our Great Adventure is over," said Fred. "We'll go to the grand opening and see the horror movies and eat at the restaurant. It'll all be fun, but it'll get normal real quick. You know—predictable."

"I'm not so sure about that," said Brother.

"What do you mean?" asked Fred.

"I recognized Igor—or whatever his real name is," said Brother.

"You did?"

"He was the supervisor of that work crew we watched from inside the barrel," said Brother. "Only he wasn't hunched over and limping then. He stood up straight and walked just like you and me. And I seem to remember a booming voice shouting orders—anyway, he sure wasn't mute."

"So what?" said Fred. "He's probably an actor playing a role. The whole thing's kind of show biz."

"I know," said Brother. "But there's something else about Igor that bothers me. He looks like someone I've seen before. Someone from the Beartown area. I just can't put my finger on who it is. Anyway, he's not who he seems to be. And then there are those workbears. Remember, they looked familiar? I think I'm having one of those premonitions you talked about...Anyway, something's wrong."

Fred liked the idea of there being a mystery about Igor and the workbears. But he didn't put much stock in it. He figured Brother was just trying to keep the excitement going.

As Fred parted company with Brother at the Bears' tree house and headed for his own home, he had no idea that the most exciting chapter of their Great Adventure had not been written yet. Or that it was about to unfold, just a few nights later, at the grand opening of Madame Bearsaud's Wax Museum and Entertainment Center.

Chapter 11
Grand Opening!

Over the next few days, Brother's suspicions increased. The more he thought about it, the more he was sure he knew that face— Igor's face. The *Beartown Gazette* claimed Igor really did hail from Grizzylvania, the legendary home of Count Bearcula. But Brother knew better. He just couldn't figure out exactly where and when he'd seen Igor before.

At last it was the evening of the grand opening. The reception was at seven o'clock in Chez Bearsaud, to be followed at eight by the opening of the wax museum. At nine there would be a showing of *Bearzilla* in the

Screaming Room. Then, at midnight, there would be a special showing of the cult rock-horror classic *The Grizzly Horror Picture Show*.

By seven-fifteen, Chez Bearsaud was packed. Waiters in costumes served drinks and appetizers. Brother and Fred took

glasses of soda from a tray held by the Frankenbear Monster. Then they were offered crackers by Queen Elizabear.

"What's that black stuff on the crackers?" Brother asked.

"Caviar," replied Queen Elizabear.

"What's caviar?" said Brother.

"It's fish eggs," said Fred.

"Uh, no thanks," said Brother. "I'll pass on the fish eggs. Got any of those little hot dogs?"

"Gullibear has those," said Queen Elizabear, "but he's tied up at the moment. Ha-ha!"

"Comedian," muttered Brother as Queen Elizabear moved off through the crowd.

"We should have taken some of those crackers," said Fred. "This is our dinner, you know."

"I got news for you," said Brother. "Those

fish eggs are spoiled. They've already turned black!"

Fred was about to tell Brother that fish eggs are supposed to be black when Madame Bearsaud's voice was heard above the din. "Ladies and gentlemen," she said into the mike she was holding, "velcome to zee grand opening of Madame Bearsaud's Vax Museum and Entertainment Center. At eight I shall open zee museum, vhere you can see Queen Elizabear's crown jewels, vhich I just took from zee safe and placed on Her Royal Highness's head. But first I vant you to see somezing just as magnificent: Lady Grizzly's priceless diamond

necklace, never before vorn in public. And here is my great and good friend now!"

As Madame Bearsaud gestured to the entrance, all eyes turned to witness the arrival of Lady Grizzly. She emerged on Squire Grizzly's arm, with a glowing smile on her face. But around her neck was something that glowed even more brightly. The priceless necklace gleamed and twinkled as it reflected the overhead lights.

The buzzing crowd had gone silent the instant the necklace had come into view. Now there was a chorus of oohs and aahs, followed by enthusiastic applause.

"Wow," said Fred to Brother. "Look at the size of those diamonds! I'll bet they're worth a gazillion!"

"More," said Brother, staring. "Two gazillion, at least!"

Lady and Squire Grizzly made their way

through the admiring crowd. Chief Bruno and Officer Marguerite followed them as closely as they could. Marguerite even had a police dog on a leash.

"Hey," said Fred, "why the police dog?"

"Maybe the chief's worried about someone stealing the necklace," suggested Brother.

"While she's wearing it?" said Fred. "And in front of everybody? Who'd be dumb enough to try that?"

All of a sudden, the lights went out. The reception was plunged into total darkness. There were a few gasps of surprise, some shuffling of feet, then a crash. The lights came back on.

"Remain calm," said Madame Bearsaud, standing by the light switch. "Zere is nuzzing wrong wis zee lights. Someone must have bumped zee switch by accident."

"What was that crash?" said Squire Grizzly.

"Something brushed against me, dear," said Lady Grizzly, "and made me drop my plate. Oh, my goodness. There's caviar all over my feet!"

The last words were barely out of Lady Grizzly's mouth when the police dog lunged forward and began licking her feet. "Ha-ha-ha!" cried Lady Grizzly. "Stop that, you brute! It tickles!"

The dog lapped up all the caviar in an instant. But then the dog did something very strange. It jumped up, put its paws on Lady Grizzly, and began to sniff at her necklace.

"Down, Spike!" said Officer Marguerite. "That's not caviar!"

"No, it isn't," said Lady Grizzly, lifting the necklace to her nose. "But—how odd—it actually smells a little like caviar...Would you have a look at this, dear?"

Squire Grizzly, who knew a thing or two about the jewelry business, sniffed at the necklace and frowned. "This isn't your necklace!" he said. "It's paste—paste with a fish glue base! It's a cheap imitation!"

"Cheap imitation?" wailed Lady Grizzly. "That means my precious necklace has been stolen!" And with that she fainted, keeling over and falling flat on her back.

Squire Grizzly reached down and patted his wife's face as Chief Bruno and Officer Marguerite rushed to his side. "Get back, folks!" barked the chief. "Give her some room!"

"She said something brushed against her!" Fred said to Brother. "Someone must have switched the necklaces while the lights were out!"

"And I think I know who it was," said Brother, looking all around. "Just before the lights went out, I saw Igor hanging around the light switch. I'll bet he turned out the lights and switched the necklaces. And now he's gone…"

"When the lights came back on," said Fred, pointing, "I noticed that door closing, as if someone had just gone through it. Let's check it out!"

Chapter 12
In the Wax Museum

When the cubs had slipped through the door, they found themselves in another large room. It was dimly lit, except for spotlights shining down on a collection of life-size wax figures of famous bears.

"It's a side entrance to the wax museum," whispered Brother. "Maybe Igor's behind one of the statues. Let's split up and check 'em out."

"Wait," whimpered Fred. "What do I do if I find him?"

"Grab ahold of his leg and scream your head off," said Brother. "I'll run and get Chief Bruno. And if *I* catch him, you do likewise."

Fred nodded, but he was trembling with fear. Brother gave him a little push, and off he went to look behind Blackbear the Pirate, Genghis Bear, and Count Bearcula. Meanwhile, Brother looked behind Queen Elizabear, Bearjamin Franklin, Gullibear, and the Frankenbear Monster.

But no Igor.

"Hey," called Fred. "There are three new statues over here! Wax statues of the Bogg Brothers! And they're perfect!"

Brother hurried over and looked. Then he took Fred by the arm and pulled him away from the statues of the Bogg Brothers. "Don't look now," he said in a hushed voice, "but they're *too* perfect."

"Huh?" said Fred, looking back at the statues.

"I said, don't look now!" said Brother. "Listen to me. Doesn't it seem odd to you that Madame Bearsaud would put statues of Billy, Bobby, and Bert Bogg, three local-yokel criminals, in her world-famous museum?"

"Now that you mention it, it does seem a little odd," said Fred. Then his eyes widened in the semi-darkness. "You mean…"

"That's right," said Brother. "Those aren't

statues. Those are the real live Bogg Brothers pretending to be statues…"

The last words out of Brother's mouth before the Bogg Brothers grabbed him and Fred and covered their mouths were, "Help, Chief!"

As if on cue, Chief Bruno burst into the room. "Back off or I'll shoot!" he cried. His pistol was pointing at Billy, the head Bogg.

"Okay, Chief, you got us," said Billy, putting up his hands. Bobby and Bert did likewise.

"All right, you three!" barked the chief. "Empty your pockets!"

Out of Bert Bogg's pocket came Queen Elizabear's pearl earrings and a ruby-encrusted bracelet. Out of Bobby Bogg's pocket came Queen Elizabear's beautiful pearl necklace. And out of Billy Bogg's pocket came...nothing.

"Turn around!" ordered the chief.

Billy Bogg turned his back to Chief Bruno.

"Well, well," said the chief. "First time I ever noticed that your backside is shaped like a crown. Come on, out with it!"

Billy pulled the crown from his pants and glared at Chief Bruno. Keeping his pistol trained on Billy, the chief turned to the cubs and said, "While I don't like to see cubs messing around with dangerous crimi-nals, I'll say this: as a policebear and as a

citizen, it does my heart good to know
we've caught the three Bogg Brothers red-
handed."

"Would you like to try for four?" came a voice from the rear. It was Officer Marguerite. She was standing in the rear exit with Igor, who was in handcuffs. And she was holding his ill-gotten gains: Lady Grizzly's priceless necklace.

"Four what?" asked Chief Bruno.

"Four Bogg Brothers," Marguerite answered. "Found him in the getaway car with the motor running."

Chief Bruno and the cubs took a good look at Igor. He was no longer shambling and bent over. And though he was taller, slimmer, and better looking than Billy, Bobby, and Bert, he looked every inch a Bogg.

"Is this guy your brother?" Chief Bruno asked Billy Bogg.

"Yep," said Billy. "As much as I hate to admit it, he's our brother Buster. Sort of the black sheep of the family. He went and became an international jewel thief." He shook his head sadly. "Don't know where we went wrong with that one."

"Okay, Marguerite," said the chief. "Cuff the rest of 'em and get them all into the police wagon."

"You know, Fred," said Brother as the Boggs were led out in handcuffs, "if I'd realized why Igor looked so familiar—just like a Bogg brother—I'd have known that those workbears were the Bogg Brothers and prevented this whole mess from happening."

"True," said Fred. "But think of it this way: one cub's mess is another cub's Great Adventure."

Brother smiled and nodded.

"Hey," said Fred, "let's go get some of that leftover food. I'm hungry."

Chapter 13
Downhill Summer

It turned out that Chief Bruno had been on the lookout for jewel thieves the moment he'd heard about Lady Grizzly's plan to wear her diamond necklace to the grand opening of Madame Bearsaud's. But he never for a minute suspected Madame Bearsaud's assistant, Igor. And neither had Madame Bearsaud.

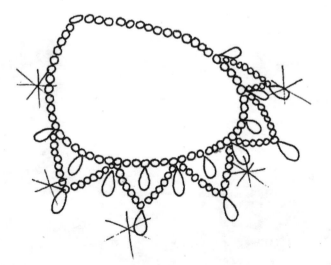

For years afterward, the grand madame was too embarrassed to tell anyone how Buster Bogg had fooled her into believing he was "Igor" from faraway Grizzylvania. But Beartown folks understood how it could have happened when they read the *Beartown Gazette*'s report on Buster Bogg's life story. Anyone who could go from a

backwater like Beartown to becoming a world-famous jewel thief had to be very clever indeed.

Brother and Fred were the talk of the town for the rest of that summer. Chief Bruno even gave them Crimestopper medals at a special ceremony in the town square. But, despite the opening of

Madame Bearsaud's Wax Museum and Entertainment Center, things sort of went downhill from there. They had more adventures, of course. But no great adventures. And certainly not another Great Adventure (the kind with a capital G and a capital A). Nothing could quite compare with watching Madame Bearsaud's building go up and sneaking in to snoop around before it opened. Not to mention helping catch a pack of jewel thieves in the middle of one of the biggest events in Beartown history.

Now *that* was a Great Adventure!

Stan and Jan Berenstain began writing and illustrating books for children in the early 1960s, when their two young sons were beginning to read. That marked the start of the best-selling Berenstain Bears series. Now, with more than one hundred books in print, videos, television shows, and even Berenstain Bears attractions at major amusement parks, it's hard to tell where the Bears end and the Berenstains begin!

Stan and Jan make their home in Bucks County, Pennsylvania, near their sons—Leo, a writer, and Michael, an illustrator—who are helping them with Big Chapter Books stories and pictures. They plan on writing and illustrating many more books for children, especially for their four grandchildren, who keep them well in touch with the kids of today.